LIGHT ME UP

A M/M LAMP ROMANCE

SABRINA CROSS

AUTHOR'S NOTE

This is a sentient object romance. Humans will be getting it on with sentient objects. Don't worry, everyone is gleefully consenting.

If you read the last three sentences and think that's not for you, that's okay. There is still time to put this book down and walk away. No one will blame you. It's the sane thing to do.

But if you're going to stick around please be aware of the following: explicit sexual activity with inanimate objects. Substance abuse, drunken behavior, dangerous activity with electric objects.

If you feel I am missing anything please reach out to me at authorsabrinacross@gmail.com and let me know. A complete list can be found at www.sabrinacross.com

NOTICES & DISCLAIMERS:

The author in no way encourages sexual activity with a lamp or any other electric appliances. Actually, they strongly discourage it and anyone who happens to get injured for trying it can no way blame the author for their own poor decision making. This is a work of fiction and not a how-to manual people. Use your brains.

CHAPTER 1
LUX

He was the first man to ever turn me on. When he flipped my switch and lit me up that first time, I knew he was it for me. There would never be another.

It was unfortunate, then, that he didn't even notice me. Sure, he appreciated my usefulness but he never really saw me when he was using me. To him, I was just another tool.

Before you get too hard on him, though, I should tell you something about myself. Something important.

I am a lamp.

Yes, you read that right.

A lamp.

Specifically, I am a studio design task light made of aluminum alloy featuring a weighted base (but don't ask me my weight), an adjustable arm with external springs, and 360-degree rotating head. Basically, I'm amazing.

I'm sure you're rubbing your head wondering how the heck I'm telling this story, but that part is easy. When I was first purchased and plugged in, before I was even used for the first time, the house was struck by lightning.

Except, it wasn't just any lightning. It was Thor's lightning. And the lightning of the gods carries with it a little bit of their power. I don't understand all of it. There's really not a manual to explain the situation. But anyway, when the power was restored to the house I woke up fully aware. I could see, I could hear, I could move around, and when I got unplugged, I was able to function for days before I finally faded to black.

Unfortunately, I unsettled the woman who owned me first with all of my exploring and testing my limits, she gave me away. I was sent to a second-hand store where I was surrounded by old things, junk, and broken objects.

I'm not sure how long I was in that place after I went black, but the next thing I knew I was being plugged in by a large, strong hand. A hand that could easily hold me too hard or force me into the slot but he didn't. And when he flicks my switch, it is always gentle. He is a large man, aware of his strength and always careful not to break me.

For me, it was love at first sight.

Jake is a student at a university. We live in a house with three other guys off-campus. When they first brought me home I was put in the living room. It was terrible there.

Some of Jake's roommates were rough with me, giving no care to how hard they flicked my switch. They often forgot to turn me off at night, though to be honest I was happy to avoid their rough touches. And once, one of them hit me with a football!

That was about the time Jake claimed me for his own and took me up to our room. He was always gentle, never left me turned on for too long, and we got to spend a lot of quality time together. I loved to watch him draw, his pen scratching along the paper or gliding across the tablet screen. His hands were magic and art in motion. I lived for the times that they were on me. I yearned for his touch in a way that was beyond anything I'd felt the whole time I'd been alive.

And he doesn't even see me.

CHAPTER 2
JAKE

ometimes I am the dumbest man known to history. This is definitely one of those times.

I wince as my arm muscles spasm, and my grip on my cock tightens. I switch arms and keep pumping, desperate to come. Again.

It started as a joke. My roommate Evan had produced a handful of pills and proposed a game. We set up half of the beer pong table, dropping pills in each cup instead of beer, and lined up.

And so it went, tossing the ball until we made one in and then downing the pill. As if that wasn't dumb enough, we hadn't stopped to ask what we were downing.

Then it began, the effects started kicking in. Sleeping pills, uppers, downers, hallucinogens, they were all there. And lucky, lucky me, so was Viagra.

The aching boner started off funny enough, but that was over an hour and four orgasms ago. Now my hand on my cock is agony but the pressure and overstimulation is better than the throbbing if I let go.

Oh, I have regrets. So many regrets. And I am

going to wring Evan's neck. Just as soon as I stop choking my cock.

"Argh!" I yell, slamming my head back on the pillow as my dick twitches and a pathetic amount of cum trickles out.

I breathe out a huge sigh and send up a prayer that it would finally be over. I wipe my hands over my face and want to weep when my dick gives no signs of going down.

"I could help you with that."

I shoot upright, looking toward the door expecting to see Evan, or maybe Dave, in the doorway. But no. It is still closed.

Fuck, I am hallucinating now. Is that a side effect of Viagra?

"Don't freak out."

My head swivels around, trying to find who is talking.

"Over here."

I jerk my gaze to the desk. My laptop is closed and the tablet screen is dark. But my lamp is on. I hadn't done that, had I? It had been off when I stumbled in. Right?

"Yes."

I jerk back, away from the desk. "Wh-what? What the fuck?"

"I told you not to freak out!" The head of the lamp tilts to the side. "I know it's weird but I could help you with that." The lamp bobs its metal head toward me, the light focused on my still erect penis.

I reach for my phone, surely hallucinations have to be a side effect of Viagra. That has to be what is happening. That makes sense.

Way more sense than a fucking talking lamp!

As the page is loading, a thud sounds from my desk. I whip my head up in time to see the lamp hopping across the surface toward me.

"What did you do, Jake?" The lamp asks softly.

Oh fuck! The lamp is talking to me and knows my name and just what? Why? Huh?

"I could tell you my story or I could help you with what looks like a very painful erection. I've never seen you so hard before."

"You," I swallow past the dryness in my throat. "You've seen me hard?"

My cock is throbbing again. I wrap my aching hand around it and squeeze, trying to relieve some pressure.

"Of course." The lamp hops closer, the arm extended toward me with the light beam still focused entirely on my dick. "Though never for so long."

Okay, I am hallucinating. That is it. I am seeing things and of course it involves my cock. My stupid, aching cock.

"That's creepy and weird." I tell the lamp. I am just going to roll with it. It is the only sane thing to do.

"Sorry." It doesn't sound sorry. "Let me make it up to you. I can help you."

"How?" It wiggles up to the very edge of the desk and its cord starts wiggling behind it.

"Wrap my cord around yourself. I'll do the rest."

It seems like a really dumb idea to wrap my erection with a power cord and like a good way to injure myself. But I am so goddamn hard and throbbing. I am so tired and my muscles are liquid.

So I do the only thing I could think to do. I yank the cord out of the wall and toward me.

"I know you like it rough but do be gentle. I'm more breakable than most of your partners."

"Sorry." Fuck me. I am apologizing to a goddamn lamp.

"Good boy," the lamp croons. "Now, wrap me

around yourself. Just like that." I loosely wrap the cord around my dick and move to prop myself against the headboard.

This is such a wild hallucination I wonder what insanity I am going to come up with next.

CHAPTER 3
LUX

can't believe this is happening! The electricity practically vibrates within me as I watch my precious Jake wrap my cord around himself. His flesh is so warm. It is soft and hard at the same time. I wonder at the feel of it.

My body trembles as he settles against the headboard. I am jerked to the very edge of the desk and have to spin around quickly to compensate for the sudden movement.

"Okay lamp, show me what you've got." Jake sounds amused as he runs his hand over my cord and his glorious cock.

"My name is Lux," I told him. "Remember that. I want to hear you scream it."

He laughs. It is a slightly wild sound that turns into a groan as I tighten my cord. I push electricity down my length until it is warm and vibrating around him.

"What the fu-" He cuts off as I squeeze tighter around him. "Oh god!"

"I'm happy to be your god." I tell him. "How does that feel?"

"So, so good." He moans, the sound vibrating

through me. My light flickers as sensation over-whelms me.

I have spent countless hours imagining what it would be like to touch Jake and to have him touch me. Of all the things I have ever imagined, it has never been anything like this.

As hot as I am, brimming with energy, Jake's skin is hotter. When I flex my cord around him again, his hand flies off the bed to grasp where I am wrapped around his cock.

I groan at the heat and pressure, sensation flooding my entire form.

"Fuck, just like that." Jake moans, pumping his hand lightly over us. "Feels so damn good."

I shove more energy down the cord, bringing it to a rapid vibration. I feel his cock twitch and flex within my grip. A few drops of pearly liquid dribble out of his tip.

I am still vibrating with sensation and emotion when Jake unwraps my cord from around his soft-ening cock.

"Finally," he says, tossing my cord next to me on the desk. "Thank god."

He looks at me and I wait for him to touch me, to stroke me, to take me to heaven. Instead, he just shakes his head and laughs under his breath.

I sink back into myself as he grabs a towel from his door knob, and leaves the room. I am still vi-brating with energy and craving his touch. But he dismisses me with a shake of his head.

My light dims and goes out as I feel my heart breaking into a million pieces.

CHAPTER 4
JAKE

ould cum on a cord short out a lamp, and other questions I am afraid to ask.

After my strange Viagra trip, I haven't plugged the cord back in for almost a week. I can hardly look at the thing without flushing red as I remember the deranged hallucination I'd had and the things I'd done.

But I need the light to work on my project for art class and now the damn thing won't turn on. Had I blown some internal fuse? Did it need a new bulb? When was the last time I replaced it?

"Oi! We're hitting The Tavern tonight," My roommate, Dave, says, coming into my doorway. "You coming? Something wrong with the lamp?"

I quickly set it on my desk and step in front of it. Rationally, I know there is no way Dave could possibly know about my momentary lamp perversion and yet I still feel myself flush.

"Nah, I have that portfolio project due Tuesday. I'll catch up with you later."

After Dave leaves, I go back to examining my broken lamp.

"What is wrong with you?" I ask, double checking the plug and trying the switch again.

"What the hell is wrong with you?" The lamp asks. I drop it on the desk and step away. It uses its head to push itself into a standing position and swivels to face me.

"What?" No. Nope. This couldn't be happening. After my misadventure with Viagra I haven't touched any substances. Not even a beer. There is no way this could be happening.

"Maybe I'm tired of being used. Maybe I don't want to be just another tool to get you off. Did you think of that?" The lamp sounds just like a disgruntled girlfriend.

"What the fuck?" I back up until I hit the bed and my knees buckle, sending me backward onto my butt. "No. No, it was just a hallucination. It wasn't real. It can't be real."

I bury my head in my hands and shake it. This isn't real. I am losing my mind. I am going crazy. Years of drinking and casual drug use must have caught up with me. Or maybe it is the pressure from school. That could cause a breakdown, right? That makes sense.

Anything makes more sense than a lamp talking to me and treating me like a bad boyfriend.

"A hallucination?" The lamp's voice is low and quiet. It almost sounds…sad? Could a lamp get sad?

"What else could it be?" I snap. There is no way I made a fucking lamp feel sad. It just isn't possible.

"Yes, that's it. I'm just a hallucination. Please don't worry about it. Just go out with your friends and by tomorrow this will all have been a crazy memory."

"You know what? That sounds like a great fucking idea." I get up and grab my phone and wallet from the desk and head out. Maybe, if I am quick enough, I can catch a ride with Dave.

"C'mon buddy, just a few more steps." Evan guides me into my room, one arm around my waist. "You're almost there, ya' idiot."

I stumble my way in the door and across the floor to my bed. When Evan would have released me, I wrap a hand around his wrist and pull him down on top of me. One hand fists into his hair, I guide his mouth to mine for a kiss.

Evan gives me one wet, sloppy kiss before shoving away from me and getting to his feet. He pulls his shirt down over his exposed abs that I kind of want to lick.

"Hell no, dude. I'm not in the mood for your limp whiskey dick. Get some sleep." He pats me on the head like the family mutt and takes off.

"I don't have a limp dick!" I yell after him, grabbing my cock through my pants and giving it a stroke. Okay, it isn't entirely hard but it won't take me long to get there.

I sit up, planning to track down Dave and see if he is up to some fun. The room tilts and spins around me like a carnival ride and I immediately lay back down and cover my face with my pillow. Evan might have a point about not being up for a good fuck right then.

"Now this is just pathetic." Comes a voice from the vicinity of my desk. I ignore it. It is fine. It am just hallucinating. I am drunk off my ass and hearing things. It happens to people all of the time.

"I thought you were done drinking yourself to oblivion after the last time. You've been so good lately."

I grumble under the pillow. There is no way I am letting a goddamn lamp judge me. So what if I am drunk? I am twenty-two-years old. I am supposed to be going out and getting drunk. It is what we do!

"So you're not even going to talk to me?" The voice is cold but a thread of sadness runs through it. It is the sadness that has me pulling my pillow away from my face and looking over at the lamp on my desk. It is perched on the very edge, the light dim and angled toward me. I wonder if the lightbulb is going bad.

"What do you want me to say? Should I apologize to my lamp for going out with the guys?" I shove upright, closing my eyes as the world tilts again. "You sound like a jealous girlfriend. You realize that is weird as hell."

"Trust me, I know how little I matter to you. I just don't want to see you kill yourself."

"Dude, you're a fucking lamp!" I wave my arms at it, emphasizing my point.

"That doesn't mean I don't have feelings!" I jerk back as the lamp yells at me.

"I bet you don't even remember my name."

I mentally flail, trying to think through the horny, orgasm-hazed memory of that night. It starts with an L. It is definitely an L name.

Why does the lamp even have a name?

"It's Lex!" I am certain of it.

The lamp growls. It fucking growls at me!

"My name is Lux, you asshole."

"You're a lamp! How do you even have a name?"

"And you're a cabbage head." The light turns off and I can hear the lamp scrape across the desk as it moves away from me.

My goddamn lamp just insulted me. Twice.

What the fuck did I do to deserve this?

CHAPTER 5
JAKE

C'mon, man. I need to work." I flip the switch off and on again but still the light remains off. Just like it has every time I've tried to use it for the last week. Ever since I forgot its – his?-- name, I've been finding the lamp in all kinds of weird places. And no matter what I try it won't ever turn on.

As absolutely crazy as it sounds, I can't deny the lamp is alive and apparently has a name and a personality. And he is really good at holding a grudge.

"Lux, I'm sorry," I run my hand along the arm of the lamp, just below the head to the joint. "You have to admit, this is a little crazy. You'll have to forgive me for not understanding or believing."

The light quivers under my touch. I do it again. It is a reaction, and more than I've gotten out of the lamp in a week. Lux's head swings slowly in my direction as the arm continues to shake beneath my hand.

"Keep doing that and I might forgive you." His voice is husky. I pause, realizing what my hand on the arm of the lamp was doing for him.

This is weird. It is really fucking weird. Then

again, so was fucking a lamp so what do I know about weird?

I wrap my hand more firmly around the upper arm and stroke downward to the joint. The light flickers on and the head falls back, directing the beam toward the ceiling.

I stroke my hand up and down the arm of the lamp with gentle, yet firm, pressure. I can feel the reverberations of Lux's groan up my arm and it immediately sears down my body to my cock. I am instantly hard. I can't help but increase the speed my hand moves. The resulting whine of energy tells me this is exactly what Lux was waiting for.

I move faster. I don't focus on the fact that I am jacking off a lamp, just on the clear sounds of pleasure I am getting from Lux. Sex sounds are one of my favorite things about sex. The moans, groans, sighs, whimpers, and shouts bring me so much pleasure.

Lux is getting brighter and brighter. I have to look away as blinding light fills the room and burns my eyes. My cock leaks pre-cum as Lux continues to whine and groan in my head. I shove my jeans down and wrap my fist around it and stroke in time to the strokes I was performing on Lux.

He is vibrating in my hand. The whine of electricity is almost deafening. I wonder how everyone in the house can't hear it. I'm close. So close. I jerk us faster and with a final groan the light goes out as Lux comes.

"No!" I yell, so close to finding my own release. My entire body tense with pleasure so good it's almost pain.

"Cord" Lux pants, feeble flickers of light flutter inside the round bulb. "Use the cord."

I yank the cord from the wall and wrap it loosely around my aching cock. It quickly heats up against my skin as Lux sends energy coursing through it. I wrap my hand around my wrapped cock and pump. The cord tightens and adds friction that has me seeing stars behind my eyelids. There is an edge of discomfort that somehow heightens the pleasure.

My balls tighten and sensation builds at the base of my cock. I am going to come. The cord heats more, a light vibration surges through it, causing my hips to buck forward. My cock throbs in my hand as cum spurts out of the tip.

I fall back onto the bed, totally spent. The cord unwinds itself from around my softening cock as I fight to catch my breath.

"Good boy." Lux croons. "But I'm not done with you yet."

I groan, unsure if I can take anymore. My body and mind spent.

CHAPTER 6
LUX

am a boiling mess of sensation and emotion. A part of me is still hurt over Jake's carelessness and disregard. Though, at some point during the last week, I realized while I've had a lot of time to process my existence, it would be shocking to someone else. I hadn't allowed Jake time to understand and accept what I am.

While I don't regret taking the time to feel my feelings and do my best to avoid Jake, it is time to forgive him. I had come to that conclusion before he began stroking me but the hand job didn't hurt.

"Lay down and take me with you." I hop to the end of the table and wait for him to pick me up. I hate that I need him to do it. I wish I could move about more on my own. I am happy to exist but being a lamp is somewhat of a mood killer right now.

But Jake doesn't hesitate to pick me up and bring me with him as he lays down. He sets me on the bed beside him and shimmies his pants down his legs and off. He is bare under his jeans, leaving his semi-hard cock fully in view. I am enjoying that, when he leans forward to yank his shirt over his head, leaving him completely bare before me.

He is lean but soft, a small cushion in his stomach that makes me want to rest my head there. A trail of light hair leads from his belly button to the curls surrounding his cock.

"Would you stop staring at me?" Jake said.

I turn to look at him and he holds a hand up over his eyes.

"Lux, light."

Funny. I didn't realize my light was on. I turn it off and nudge his leg with my base.

"Take out my bulb." I say, leaning toward him. I can do it myself. I found that out quite by mistake in the early days. My bulb had laid on the table for hours before my owner got home and replaced it. That was the final straw for her, and what eventually led me to my Jake. Yes, I could do it myself, but I want Jake to.

Jake's hands are gentle as he grasps my bulb and turns. I gasp. It never felt that good when I turned it myself. His hands are so soft, so good.

He must know what it is doing to me because the quick, economical movement slows down and the turning becomes more of a caress.

"This is by far one of the weirdest things I've ever done." Jake says to me, finally pulling my bulb free from the socket. He looks at the bulb in his hand and then back at me. "What now?"

"Suck it." I can't feel it. Once the bulb is removed I lose sensation, but I want to see a part of me inside of him.

"That doesn't seem safe." He eyes the bulb warily. But it isn't a no.

"Baby, I'm a hopping, talking lamp. I am infused with the power of Thor. My glass is unbreakable."

Slowly he raises the bulb to his mouth as I watch, waiting for the moment it hits his lips, before lowering my head and taking the tip of his cock into my socket. He jolts, shoving his cock deeper. I send a tingling level of electricity through him.

"Oh, fuck!" He thrusts his hips up against me. "That's, uh, oh!"

My socket is only deep enough to take his head but I take as much as I can. I begin to fluctuate energy levels from a soft, gentle hum to an intense buzz. His hand wraps tightly around the bottom of my arm just above the base. For a moment I worry he is going to pull me away but then his other hand wraps around the base of his own shaft, holding it tightly as I buzz around him.

"Oh, my God." Jake groans.

"I am a god, but I don't believe I am your god." A deep voice says from the doorway.

CHAPTER 7
JAKE

jerk in shock and am relieved when Lux pulls away from me. I grab a pillow to cover my junk before looking at the man standing in the door. He is tall, his head almost brushing the frame. He is built, blonde, and wearing a tailored suit. His blue eyes are bright, almost glowing.

Beside me Lux swings around to stare at the man as well. At least I assume that's what he is doing. I really wish he had an actual face.

"What the fuck?" I say, not getting up but wishing I was wearing pants and hadn't just been caught fucking my lamp. "Who the fuck are you and why are you in my room?"

"I'm not here for you mortal." He waves a dismissive hand and look at Lux. "I've been looking for you, my little friend."

Lux quivers beside me. It isn't from lust like it had been before. He is scared. I can feel it coming off of him in waves.

"I've been here." Lux says, his tone defiant.

"Yes, and you shouldn't be." The man steps forward, reaching for Lux. The lamp cowers back, pushing closer to me. "You know you don't belong here."

Lux says nothing. I pick him up and set him on my lap, wrapping my arms around him.

"He's mine. You can't have him." Protectiveness surges through me. I don't know who this man is, but he isn't taking Lux from me. Not now. Not ever.

"He shouldn't even exist." The man says, taking another step forward.

"And yet he does." I may not understand his existence but Lux is a person. He has thoughts and feelings and I'd be damned if I let anyone take him from me. "You're not touching him."

The man pauses, looking from me to Lux and back again. His head cocks to the side as he eyes us. I'm sure we look a sight. I am sitting naked on my bed covered only by a lumpy grey pillow and hugging a rather tall table lamp.

"Interesting." The man said. "Very interesting. And you lamp?"

"My name is Lux." Lux spits out. I grin and hug him tighter. "I'm not going anywhere. I belong here. You may have made me but you can't control me."

"Very interesting." The man, who I am now realizing may actually be a god, grins. "You know, this happens from time to time. My energy goes wild and something gets caught up in it. But in all my centuries I've never had one of these creatures become so sentient. It's like he's his own being."

"That's because he is."

"Hmmm." Thor, he has to be Thor, cocks his head to the side. "The lamp thinks and feels. How interesting."

"Will you stop referring to him as a lamp? He is a person." Okay, fine, maybe I had been referring to him as a lamp too, but I know better. Lux is his own being, and he is as real as anyone.

"You defend it. This is fascinating." The man

grins. "You know, I had come to fix my mistake. It's never good for inanimate objects to gain sentience. They never seem to know what to do with it and it always ends poorly. But I think in this case I'm going to make an exception."

"I get to stay?" Lux asks, his voice barely a whisper.

"You get to stay, little one." Thor moves forward again, and I hug Lux tighter to my chest. "Give me the lamp, boy. I promise I'll do him no harm."

I look to Lux, who gives a brief nod. I don't trust the god and it feels wrong to hand Lux over to him but I decide to trust Lux. It will be okay. It has to be.

As soon as Lux is in Thor's hands there is a bright, blinding flash of light. I look away and cover my eyes but can still see an afterimage of white. I am still blinded when a laugh tears through the room.

I look toward Thor, blinking to regain sight. But Thor is gone. In his place is a man about my age. He is lean and angular with fair blond hair and light silvery eyes. He stands naked in the center of my room running his hands over himself. It isn't sexual but more the act of someone trying to learn the feel of something.

"What? Who?" I stammer out, unable to take my eyes off of the guy.

"It's me." The guy says. I recognize the timber of the voice immediately.

"Lux?" I can't believe it. I look around trying to find the lamp, certain it had to be a trick but the lamp is gone and there is only this human left. "Holy shit."

"Thor gave me a gift." He steps forward and pauses, his eyebrows drawn down and his eyes clouded. "He told me I could stay or that he would find somewhere for me to go."

"Stay." I say, before the words even processed in my brain. "Stay with me."

Lux launches himself at me. His mouth comes to mine in a fierce kiss and his arms wrap around my shoulders. My mind is reeling from everything that just happened but this kiss, it's perfect. It is just right.

CHAPTER 8
LUX

He was the first man to ever turn me on. When he flipped my switch and lit me up that first time, I knew that he was it for me. There would never be another.

It is fortunate for me Jake feels the same. It is a dream come true. It is everything I had never dared to wish for. It is somehow my very real life now. And I feel like I could burst from happiness.

Thor set me up with an identity, some money, and an apartment. It isn't enough to live on forever, but it is enough to get me started. I enrolled in college to become an electrician. Even though I am no longer a lamp I can still feel electricity in a way I soon realized others couldn't. Jake and I figure being an electrician is a good way to put that talent to use.

As soon as he found someone to take over his room, Jake moved in with me. It isn't perfect. It turned out Jake is kind of a mess, and both of us hate doing dishes and taking out the trash. There has been more than one night I worry arguments over such things will be enough to make him leave. But he never does.

"You're an idiot." He'd tell me. "I stood up to a

literal god to keep you and you think an argument or dishes is going to be enough to drive me away?"

That usually ends up with us fucking on whatever surface was handy. Jake is even more insatiable than I ever realized during those months watching him with various hookups. Though we never talked about that or the people who came before me. It doesn't bother me I wasn't his first and that I'd seen him with others, but Jake says it creeps him out a little bit to know I was watching. I'm sure why but I'm happy to respect his wishes and pretend it never happened.

Is it happily ever after? Who could say? But I am determined to do my best to enjoy the life I was unexpectedly given and to love the man I never thought would see me.

ACKNOWLEDGMENTS

First and foremost I want to thank everyone who has made it this far. Thank you for coming along on this very weird journey with me and I hope you enjoyed reading Lux and Jake as much as I enjoyed writing them. I also hope you forgive me for taking a brief break from Yarn and Monsters to put this out in the world. Anything that exists beyond Corny only exists because of you and your support. Please know that every like, comment, review, silly gif, or post you make means the world to me. I wish I could give you each a giant, squishy hug. But that would probably be weird for all of us.

It takes a village to write a book, at least the way I do it, and I've got a great village. Josh, Amy, & Ellie thanks for letting me geek out about my writing even though you don't always understand or care. Cate and Liz, thanks for taking me seriously even when I don't usually take myself seriously. Thanks to the Black Hat Coven for endless support and cheerleading and just generally brightening my day.A big, huge, whopping thanks to Brittany Egles and Writer's Wingman editing for taking the sloppy chaos and making it make sense. And for letting me panic text you "I forgot how to write" all hours of the day. If I'm a success in any way it's only because of you.

To Mom & Dad - I told you I'd use that writing degree some day. I don't think any of us saw "Lamp Smut" coming but hey, life's a journey.

ABOUT THE AUTHOR

Sabrina Cross (she/her) is a neurospicy 80's baby from the middle of nowhere Michigan, where she still lives with her cat. She came into her monster romance era early when she fell in love with Beast from the 1997's X-Men animated series. After discovering sentient object romance in early 2023, Sabrina decided to embrace what she calls her 'Hold My Beer' style of writing and gave into the lifelong dream of being an author. When not writing weird monster/sentient object smut, Sabrina can be found hanging out on social media (@authorsabrinacross), reading, or hoarding office supplies.

ALSO BY SABRINA CROSS

Yarn & Monsters Series

A True Love Spell Gone Wrong...

When four friends perform a true love spell, things go terribly wrong. Now they're locked into a deal with the devil and have only a year to find love and happiness or their souls are destined to face the flames. Armed with a demon guardian; Clover, Jasmine, Fern, and Violet are determined to beat the devil and save themselves. Except, this curse might be the best thing that's ever happened to them.

Corny: A F/F Candy Corn Romance

A True Love Spell Gone Wrong…

A Demon Fairy Godmother?

Her very soul on the line. Can Clover still find true love or is she destined to face the flames alone?

Snuggle: A M/F Demon Teddy Bear Romance

A True Love Spell Gone Wrong…

Jasmine is too busy to go to Hell and she's definitely too busy for demon antics. But when her demon "Fairy Godmother" shows up, everything is on the line. Does she have what it takes to get out of the Devil's bargain or is she doomed to face the flames?

Tangled: A M/F Friends-To-Lovers Sentient Object Romance

A True Love Spell Gone Wrong…

Fern is going to Hell. Not metaphorical Hell but actual, physical Hell. But there's one thing she needs to do before she goes. An item she desperately needs to scratch off the bucket list. And she's hoping the demon sent to guard her will be willing to help her out.

Knotted: A M/F Demon Werewolf Romance

A True Love Spell Gone Wrong…

Violet was no witch but that didn't stop her from trying to use magic to find love. When the spell backfired and left her and her friends bound in a deal with the devil, Violet vowed to find a solution. Now, with less than two months until the deal comes due and zero leads, she's facing the fire. The fire comes early in the form of a great black beast in her bed. Does Violet find the love she's been looking for or does Hell claim her soul?

Light Me Up

He was the first man to ever turn me on. When he flipped my switch and lit me up that first time, I knew he was it for me. There would never be another.

Pounded by the Pommel Horse

Elena loves being on top. When the elite gymnast is challenged to defeat her gym rival on the pommel horse, she's up for the task. But is she up for the ride when the pommel horse shapeshifts into a man? A very, very naked Man?

Christmas with the Monster

He's Got a Package for Her… Devynn expected her first holiday without her kids to be difficult. But nothing could have prepared her for what she found under the tree just after midnight.With the help of his magic sack, the furry, green giant promises Devynn all kinds of pleasure. But would one night with the Christmas monster ever be enough?

Sentient Pen15 from Outer Space

Liam had spent a lot of his childhood obsessed with the legends of the local mines. The abandoned tunnels underground had driven dozens of workers insane and young Liam was desperate to get to the bottom of it. But he found more than he bargained for down there.

Infected by parasitic space mold, Liam has held himself away from relationships for years. When things spark between him and the girl next door, he has no choice but to reveal the truth: his manly appendage is also the bane of his existence.

The Glory Whole Package

Never Piss Off a Witch.

It is a hard-learned lesson and one I may never complete. The endless boredom of my curse is only broken by analyzing the people who use me.

Today I break my silence for the first time and while it might lead to a Happily Ever After, it will never be mine. Not until I've paid for my crimes and earned the forgiveness of the only person I've ever loved.

Getting Railed

"Welcome to Retro Whimsy!"

I hadn't planned on buying anything when entering the new vintage store during my lunch break but somehow found myself leaving with a toy train set.

What could have been written off as an impulse purchase became so much more when those trains come to life.

Now I'm stuck dealing with the consequences of a god curse and deciding if I have what it takes to help break it.

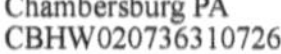